WIND

Charleston, SC
www.PalmettoPublishing.com

WIND

Copyright © 2021 by Ranger Dollins

All rights reserved.

No portion of this book may be reproduced, stored in a retrieval system, or transmitted in any form by any means–electronic, mechanical, photocopy, recording, or other–except for brief quotations in printed reviews, without prior permission of the author.

First Edition

Paperback ISBN: 8-1-63837-828-0

WIND

a short thriller by
RANGER DOLLINS

Daryl

"Breathe, just breathe." He lights a cigarette, hands shaking with nerves. Sweat forming on his brow. This is always the worst part of any "job", the moments before, his mind racing with possibilities of what could go wrong. Could I get caught? Go to prison? Die? These thoughts always plague his mind before what he calls "work". Then he thinks of what would happen if he didn't do the job, if he didn't get any money, if he didn't get that next hit... He thinks back to the start of his addiction. Before Daryl worked on the pipeline in West Texas, long days of sweat, grime, dust. After working like a dog all week under the hot Texas sun, taking orders from men Daryl fancied himself "smarter than" he would be dying to go out on the town. To run the streets and paint the town, let his wild streak come out and breathe. He would go out with his friends to party, dance, and meet girls. That's when his tumultuous relationship with Cocaine started. At first it was just a fun thing to do on the weekends, help blow off a little steam here and there. Not a big deal as long as he only used it occasionally, until he didn't. Until he started using daily, after work, at night when he should be sleeping, before shift, during shift. And when he tried to quit, his ears would ring louder and louder, as if a dog whistle was planted in his ear slowly but surely hollowing out his brains while his skin crawled and itched. His head would pound and pound for days on end, hours felt like years until he finally took a hit. But he had a good job so he could afford his addiction and keep it to himself for the most part. Until the White House decided that oil was no longer an acceptable form of energy and pipelines across the state were shut down. With dwindling funds and worsening withdrawals, Daryl turned to the East Texas Killer for help, Methamphetamine. That first hit was like heaven in a bag, life giving energy he so desperately needed. A pulsating high that brought him back from the dead, pulling him straight out of the grave and putting him back on his feet. With no education and little work around home he turned to crime to pay for his hits. It wasn't his first time, Daryl had been in and out of trouble his whole life. The son of an abusive alcoholic father, Daryl would often get into trouble as a kid just to stay away from home a little longer. The only lesson his dad ever really taught him was to fend for himself, by any means necessary, a lesson he took to heart. So stealing for drug money was never a big deal to him. It started small, robbing houses for money, sometimes people on the wrong side of town for whatever they had on them at the time. But things escalated as his ambition and desperation grew; in the last year he's robbed three banks, small ones albeit. Today's different though, today's target is a Commercial Bank Of Texas in Nacogdoches, Texas. A bigger bank, but a bigger pay day.

His old, beat up truck looks out of place outside the tall red brick building with its large white columns out in front. The building itself embodies a daunting task. It's in a nicer part of town and reflects that in its size and beauty. The clock strikes 9 A.M.. "Time for work" he says with a smirk, as he throws out his cigarette and pulls his ski mask over his long hair and short beard. *I hate this thing*, he thinks to himself. *Always messes up my moustache.* He pulls his truck in front of the tall, tower-like doors to the bank. The glass is tinted solid black, he has no clue what awaits him on the other side, death or glory? He leaves the truck running as he gets out, his heart pounds as he approaches. Every decision he ever made led him here to this fateful moment. He walks into the bank gun in hand. He takes a second to scope out the inside of the bank, a big open floor with tall ceilings and columns. Granite floors and a tall marble counter. Only a rich man would keep money in a place like this, its open design makes him feel like a small fish in a big tank, swallowing him up in it's vastness. Daryl takes a breath and clears his throat.. "HELLO LADIES AND GENTS! This here is a robbery!" Only four people are in the bank this early, an elderly couple and a young man in line behind them wearing a ball cap. They all look at him with wide eyes and slowly raise their hands. Daryl walks past them to the counter "Everybody relax and don't forget to breathe, I'm here to rob the bank, not you." he says with a smile. He looks at the employee behind the counter, a young Mexican girl with dark, coarse hair and brown eyes like jars of honey. "Y'all got a vault round here sweetheart?" "We do but I don't know the code for it." she says with a shaky voice, her eyes wide open, her complexion turning a shade of white. Daryl sighs loudly, then quickly points his revolver in her face. "Don't die for someone else's money kid" She nods her head and takes him to the back room, he clears out the register and puts all the money in his bag first. "Now while I'm in this room I'm gonna need all y'all to lay on the floor with your face down so I know you're not misbehaving while I'm gone." "You ought to be ashamed son," says the old man. He peers at Daryl with withered blue eyes from under his cowboy hat. Daryl turns and approaches the old man, clomping his boots slowly on the way there. "Do yourself a favor, oldtimer, and shut the hell up, get your ass on the ground or I'll open your head up all over this floor," he says with a grin. Daryl no longer feels the nerves or the anxiety of before, now he only feels power. He's oozing charisma at this point, completely in the moment and enjoying every bit of it. Soaking it all in. The old man complies, still glaring at Daryl. His wife and the other guy are already on the ground. Daryl looks at the young man on the ground, with his face looking away from everyone. "What about you boy? Got anything stupid to say as well?" No reply. "HUH? You got cotton in your ears kid?" Daryl asks, gripping his gun tightly. The young man turns his face and looks at Daryl, "No Sir" he says quietly. "Well good deal, least one of you's got a brain in yer head." Daryl enters the back room with the girl from the bank. It's a small room, walls barren and not much to look at, but in the back corner lies a huge vault. It's tall and black as night, with a big wheel handle on the front. Daryl's heart skips a beat just seeing it. The girl turns and looks at Daryl with anxious eyes. "There's not much in there, just enough to give out small loans." Daryl drops his shoulders and rolls his eyes, "I don't care about the details honey, just open the frickin thing up please." He says in a pleading tone. She enters the code on the keypad, hands shaking and breathing heavy. "Error", the small screen shows. "C'mon kid pull yourself together." Says Daryl. "I'm sorry, I don't know if I can remember the code." Her voice breaks as her eyes swell with tears. Daryl grabs her hand and holds it on the keypad, looking deep into her eyes. "It's okay, just breathe. I ain't gonna hurt you, I promise." She takes a deep breath, inhale, exhale. She puts in the code one more time. The safe unlocks. Daryl opens the door, his eyes open as wide as his mask will let them, his jaw dropping to his belt buckle. Tall stacks of cash banded together sit in the safe, at least a dozen of them. "Thank you god for this life of sin." He says with a smirk. *It's got to be at least 30k, he thinks.* Daryl starts throwing money in his backpack while the girl holds it for him. His shoulders squared up, head held high, feet lighter than they've been in a while. This is why he does it, sure he needs a hit, but the swell of dopamine rushing his brain is what keeps him in this line of "work". The Adrenaline, the excitement, this is the only place where he's fully in control of himself and the world around him. Outside these walls he might be just another junkie, but in here with a gun in his hand Daryl is whoever he chooses to be. He might as well be god in his eyes. "Why do you do this?" asks the girl. "You're going to get caught eventually, so why even try?" Daryl looks at her and laughs, "Cause it's fun!" He zips up his bag which is crammed tight with money and walks out of the door of the vault room. "Did yall miss me!?" POW POW! Daryl falls behind the bank counter. "AHHH!!" Daryl shouts in pain. He rips his mask off his head to get some air, he's been shot once through his abdomen, the second shot just grazed his hip. Bloods rushing out of his wound turning his light grey button up shirt a dark red. Bullets are ripping through the counter, throwing chunks of marble and granite through the air, papers and money falling all around Daryl while he tries to get his witts back. The girl from the bank lies motionless on the ground, a stray bullet passed through her head as she tried to duck for cover. Daryl's eyes fixate on her, blood slowly runs out of her head. The look on her face is almost one of sadness, as if she had been heartbroken. The ringing in Daryl's ears is deafening, his heart pounding out of his chest, he breathes quickly and heavily. He looks away from the girl, and holds his wound, *No time to be upset,* he thinks, *This is on you.* The gunfire stops, he can hear someone fumbling a gun and its magazine. *Someone's reloading,* he thinks to himself; this is his only chance to get out alive. His stomach aches with dread, *I've never killed anyone before,* he thinks. It's the last thing he wants to do right now, but in his mind there's no other option; he won't go to prison, he's already decided that. With one hand on his wound and the other on his gun, he jumps up from behind the counter pointing his gun, he scans the room for a threat. The old couple are lying on the ground covering their heads, the old lady is crying aloud. Then he hears the slide of a pistol rack, it's the young man from the back of the line. He's taken cover behind one of the granite columns. Daryl points his 357 Mag. revolver at the column. POW POW! Chunks of granite explode out of the back of the column, "UGH" The young man runs out from the Column with blood all over his shirt, his eyes wired open, teeth grit in agony. He raises his gun at Daryl and fires four times while moving across the room, Daryl runs sideways in the opposite direction firing three shots. All three rip through the boy's body, he crumples to the ground like a lifeless bag. Daryl stands in disbelief of what just happened, sweat pouring down his face, arms and legs shaking. He quickly reloads his gun and grabs his backpack full of money and limps as fast as he can for the door; his truck is parked right outside if he can just make it there. He crashes into the bank doors swinging them wide open. "DROP THE GUN!" A sheriff's deputy twenty feet away points his gun at Daryl. Daryl raises his gun and fires without hesitation, POW POW! He misses and the Deputy returns fire. Daryl ducks behind his truck, bullets slapping the side of the cab. He crawls towards the bed while the deputy shoots through the doors of the single cab truck. *Damn it, he must have heard the shots from the bank while driving by,* he thinks to himself. It's so humid; the Texas sun cooks the moist spring air making it thick and heavy. Daryl's covered in blood and sweat, still gasping for breath, his brain working on overdrive. He peeks under the truck and sees the Deputies legs, which are moving to the front of Daryl's truck. Daryl knows what the Deputy is doing, he's closing distance and getting ready to eliminate the threat. Daryl jumps up from the back side of the truck and fires two rounds through the back glass and windshield into the deputy, who now stands in front of the hood of the truck. The Deputy falls backwards onto the ground with a grunt. Daryl rushes forward, gun in hand pointing it at the bloodied officer who is reaching for his gun he dropped on the ground. "DON'T!" Daryl yells at him. He's so close to the wounded deputy he can see the whites of his eyes and the sweat on his face. *Please don't,* he thinks. The deputy glances at Daryl just for a second, and then grabs his gun and tries to point it at him. BANG! Daryl fires his last bullet and cuts through the deputies head, who now lies lifeless on the ground with eyes still open. "Shit." He throws his money bag in the truck and jumps in, he gasps in pain as he sits on shattered glass, digging into the bottom of his legs. He tears out of the parking lot, and even though he got the money and escaped, he feels hopelessly defeated.

The feelings of control and power are long gone, along with any chance of returning to "normal life" although normal might be different for Daryl than most people. His truck roars through town, weaving in and out of traffic and running red lights. People driving by and walking on the sidewalk all stare at the battered truck as he flies by them. *Just get off the main roads, get out of town and drive around the big towns.* Suddenly his heart drops and he gets a raw feeling in the pit of his stomach, in the opposite lane of the highway heading right towards him are three police cars, sirens blaring. He turns his head away from them, his gun in hand. Time moves at a stand still as they get closer and closer, his hands gripping the wheel with a white knuckle grip. They drive right past him. He breathes a sigh of relief and heads towards the country. He drives with his shoulders slouched and his head down, his hair falling into his eyes, covered in granite powder and blood. Tears trickle out of his eyes, his insides feel knotted up, twisted, and broken. He flies down the road, face blood red, trembling, holding everything in. He feels as if his insides are going to implode from the turmoil inside himself, his whole body writhing and shaking in pain, but not from the external wound. He's been driving for half an hour now towards Tyler, TX. He pulls over on the shoulder and begins to softly cry, which turns to weeping, and then screaming. "AHHHHHHH. What's wrong with YOU?! The hell's wrong with you?!" He screams as he hits the steering wheel. He melts into the seat sobbing aloud, eyes gazing up at the heavens. "Why God? Why did you make me like this? WHY?!" He cries and moans, the face of the bank girl torturing his mind. He pulls his gun out and loads a single bullet into it and looks at the weapon for a few seconds, anxiously deliberating. He then puts it in his mouth, finger on the trigger. His breathing heavy, chest swelling in and out with air. Sweat dripping off his hair onto the gun, blood still draining out his wound. His whole body trembles and aches with dread. He shuts his eyes and counts to three. One . . . Two . . . Three . . . He hesitates, slowly opens his eyes and looks out of the passenger side window. tall green grass fills the ditch of the desolate farm to market road. Strong gusts of April wind sway the branches of the tall East Texas timber, like a friend waving in the distance. Bright yellow springtime daisies cover every pasture. It's quiet. Dark clouds are rolling in from the south, the air is so thick he can taste it. He Deeply exhales. Pulls the gun out of his mouth and sets it aside. *I coulda done anything with my life, and I chose to do this.* He looks at the bag of money in the passenger seat, maybe I can still be someone else. He puts the truck in drive and gets back on his way. All that matters now is getting away, sticking to farm to market and county roads, avoiding the main highways. With this much money he could start over, something small and honest. All the death today wouldn't have to be for nothing. He heads west with the sun.

Daniel

"Breathe, Just breathe. I'm not gonna hurt ya." Daniel peers into the eyes of a young man, a scrappy looking kid, his jeans and T-shirt covered in dirt and sweat. Daniel approaches him from across the small blank room. "I know what you did last week here in Amarillo Jesse." "I haven't done anything sir," he replies nervously. Daniel continues to stare through the man, his cold, green eyes fixated on his suspect. "Is that right?" "Yes," Jesse replies. "You didn't break into the Bodark's home and kill Mr. Bodark and his fifteen year old boy?" Daniel says in a loud skeptic tone while squinting his eyes. "No!" Jesse replies, face pointed towards the ground. "We found your blood at the scene of the crime Jesse, I guess they put up more of a fight than you expected," he says with a smirk. "I get it, I do, you bust up in the house around noon on a Monday, not really expecting anyone to be there. Just trying to steal enough for drug money. Then the residents get home early and you flip out and butcher them with a kitchen knife." Jesse nervously looks away from Daniel, his frizzy hair partially hiding his eyes. He looks around the room scanning it, a small, square interrogation room, with just one small window. "There's no way outta here boy," says Daniel with a smile. "Who are you again?" asks Jesse. "I'm Texas Ranger, Daniel Haze, and if I'm investigating you, just know that you're screwed." "I ain't hurt nobody." Daniel chuckles and slowly walks across the room, dragging his boots across the floor. His tall, broad build making Jesse look like a small child next to an angry parent. He rests one arm against the wall Jesse's standing against, the other hand on his holstered pistol, and leans forward, so close that his cowboy hat is poking into Jesse's hair. He takes one hand and fixes the ends of his moustache, still glaring at Jesse whose eyes are now fixed on the ground. "Do you believe in God?" Daniel asks him. "Yes sir." "You shouldn't. There might be a God outside for you, but in these walls there's only one god, me" says Daniel with a crooked smile. "I make the rules in here, boy. You don't do anything without my permission. I decide where you go, what you eat, when you sleep, what time you get up, when you get to take a piss. I giveth and I taketh away. I am your God." Daniel swells his chest and leans even closer to the boy; he enjoys these moments, perhaps too much. He specializes in interrogation, one of the state's best. At the age of thirty five he's made a name for himself all across the west, the Texas Rattlesnake they call him. He thinks back to when he was a kid, his alcoholic father used to beat him and his little brother almost every day, albeit he didn't get it near as bad as his younger brother did. He peers deeper into Jesse's eyes; he often sees his father's eyes in his suspects. "Hmh," Daniel scoffs at the boy; he feels power in these moments. Power that he so desperately craved as a scared little boy. He pulls his gun out and points it at Jesse's stomach. "What are you doing?" says Jesse with a shaky voice. "What? Are you getting scared?" Jesse looks Daniel in his eyes for the first time in the interrogation. "You're a lawman, you can't do that!" Daniel snickers at him. "Do what? There ain't no cameras in this room, Nobody on the other side of that glass cares if I shoot you." Jesse's eyes widen as the color drains from his face, his breathing light and fast. Daniel presses the gun into Jesse. "But maybe a bullet's too good for you, maybe I should stab you to death like you did that man and his boy. Did they beg when you killed them? Did they cry? Did you enjoy killing them like I'm gonna enjoy killing you?" Suddenly the door to the room flies open, "Stand down Haze!" yells the police chief. "Piss off." Daniel says, his gaze still on the boy. "That's an order Haze." "I said piss off Chief, or I'll arrest you for interfering in a state investigation." The chief shakes his head and leaves the room while dialing a number on his phone, shutting the door behind him. Daniel redirects his attention to Jesse. "What did you do to that family Jesse?" Tears swelling in Jesse's eyes, face beat red. "I didn't know they would be home!" Jesse drops to his knees and erupts into tears. "I didn't want to." Jesse chokes out while sobbing on the floor. Daniel holsters his 1911 Pistol and motions at the glass for the officers to take him away. "Thank you for your confession son, I'm sure God hears you" he says sarcastically on his way out. "You're gonna be in trouble for that one Haze," says a female officer as he passes by. "Wouldn't be the first time," he replies.

    He leaves the building and walks outside to light a cigarette. He walks to the edge of the parking lot and looks down over Amarillo while lighting his cigarette. He gazes into the distance watching the sun set over the Texas panhandle. He pulls out his phone and sees two missed calls, one from his ex-wife, and another from an old friend in the force from Nacogdoches. Glaring at the screen, he debates who to call first. It's been years since his divorce but not a day goes by that he doesn't think of her, *My South Texas dream* he used to call her. Wind gusts across the parking lot, blowing dust through the air, it howls and sings as the sun disappears behind the horizon. The Panhandle reminds Daniel of his own isolation, and after a moment of debate he flicks his cigarette and lets out a sigh. He scrolls past his ex-wife and calls his friend from Nacogdoches, maybe some other time he tells himself. The phone rings twice and is immediately answered. "Mark, what the hell you want man, I'm busy." Daniel says with a smile. "Daniel, I'm sorry I tried to call earlier, there was a bank robbery today in town." Mark says in a dreadful tone "Alright, what about it?" "The suspect killed two, possibly three people, one of them was Allen." Daniel freezes at the words and stands in silence. "I'm sorry, we got there and the suspect had already escaped. He's seriously wounded and on the run, it's only a matter of time before we find him." " I'm in Amarillo, I'll go ahead and drive to Gainesville right now and catch a few hours of sleep. I'll be in Nacogdoches by tomorrow morning." Daniel says with a sigh. "Don't push yourself too hard Daniel, we'll catch this guy by the end of this week." Mark replies. "I aint worried about that," says Daniel. "I need to see Allen's family, they must be in pieces." "Alright then, you be careful." "same to you Mark, thanks for the call." Daniel ends the call with a lump in his throat, he fights back tears as he lets out a cough. After a moment he gathers himself and pushes his emotions back down inside. Allen was his first partner when he became a Nacogdoches police officer at twenty years old. They had been on some of their worst calls together, always had each others back. When Daniel's first child died a week after she was born, it was Allen and his family that were there for Daniel and his wife. When Allen lost his personal car to the repo man, Daniel went and bought it back for him. Daniel stands silent for a moment, memories of his friend running laps around his brain. Wonderful memories all tainted by an untimely murder. He wipes the tears from his face and takes a deep breath. He pulls his phone back out and texts Mark. "Do you have a name for the suspect?" "Only a first name so far." Mark replies. "What is it?" asks Daniel. A moment goes by, no reply yet. Daniel has a sinking feeling in the bottom of his stomach, a dread that can't be subdued, or reasoned with. Like regretting a decision before you've even made it. As if he's seen lightning and is waiting on the thunder to shake the house. His mouth is dry, hands clammy, he can't understand why he feels so sick, it's almost as if it were instinctual, primal, coming from somewhere deep within the subconscious corners of his mind. Another strong gust of wind blows. His legs feel weak, like he just ran a marathon, like he just hiked up a mountain, for a control freak like him the sensation is dizzying. Nauseating. Cracks are showing in his armor, his bravado is failing him, he's glad he's alone right now, he wouldn't want anyone to see him break. The phone vibrates in his hand and lights up. His heart jumps, then drops. He reads the message. "Daryl"

Denouement

"Breathe, keep breathing." With every breath a sharp nauseating pain rips through Daryl's side; his wound still leaking blood, although the old T-shirt he tied around it has helped slow the bleeding a good bit. It's midnight, and he's exhausted from hours of driving down curvy, winding back roads. The plan has worked so far, he hasn't run into any cops or nosy drivers. But now even the simple task of driving requires all his focus; his eyes glazed over and a shade of yellow. He slouches forward in his bloody seat with both hands gripping the top of the wheel, back aching from top to bottom. He stopped for gas once just outside of Tyler, but the truck's running on fumes again, and he needs a rest. He's just west of Gainesville now and looking for a small, isolated place to fuel up. Winding down the long twisted road, the truck shakes and groans, as if it were begging for rest as well. The road he's on climbs and falls with the rolling hills of the western landscape. Daryl's mind roams aimlessly with the land he traverses, thinking of events, people, and places he's been. Past and present run together in a dizzying mesh of memories and ideas. The events of this morning are particularly heavy on his mind, playing on repeat over and over. The gun shots, the noise, the rush and thrill, the girls face. He thinks of every moment in his life that led him to where he is at now, and searches for someone to blame. At first he blames his father, the beatings and neglect he suffered at his hands. He blames his father for never teaching him how to be a man, for never giving him anything but anger and no way to deal with it. Then he blames his big brother, for leaving home the first chance he got and never coming back for him, leaving Daryl to fend for himself. "He could have taken me with him." Then finally Daryl blames society itself for placing it's unattainable expectations on him. Expectations of success, expectations of morality, and expectations of what a man should be. The definition of a man always puzzled and frustrated him. A man has to work and provide, be tough but not too hard. Be gentle but not too soft. A man has to be caring but not weak, good but also a little bad. A man has to be a visionary but also ever present and never distracted, a man has to be day and night. It's enough pressure to make anyone crack, he thinks. Angry sentiments bounce around his brain like wrecking balls in a building, but he knows where the anger should be directed, despite a bad hand in life, he knows he only has himself to blame for his current circumstances.

   He pulls out his last smoke and lights it, the nicotine soothes his brain, calming his thoughts. The smoke glides and dances within the cab of the truck, until being sucked out through the shattered back glass. A quiet country tune plays on the radio, the sad, steel guitar moaning along the lonely highway. The night is cold, not in temperature but in nature. Dark clouds roll through with a strong wind, covering up a crescent moon. The wind whips and beats the prairie grass, throwing it side to side, flashes of lightning far to the north, so far away there's no thunder to be heard with it. No animals calling out to the moon, just .. silence. Lights appear ahead up the road, Daryl's eyes squint to make out what it is, dreading what it could be. His heart leaps, a gas station, small and dimly lit atop a grassy hill overlooking the prairie. A black truck sits next to one of the pumps. Daryl scopes it out, no cops, probably just someone needing gas. He'd rather not stop with someone else around but his fuel gauge is on empty, so he pulls in to the only other pump. He scans the parking lot from the inside of the truck, his blood shot eyes checking for danger. No one seems to be around, whoever's in the black truck must be asleep. Daryl exit's his truck and starts fueling up, keeping his head on a swivel the whole time. Something feels wrong in the air, he doesn't know what but he wants to leave as soon as possible. He hears someone get out of the black truck behind him. Daryl places his hand on his hip and feels his gun, just in case he needs it. The pumps of the old gas station move excruciatingly slowly. Daryl peeks over his shoulder to try and see who's behind him. All he can see is a cowboy hat sticking out from behind the pump. The stranger lets out a cough and starts pumping gas. Daryl turns his attention back to the pump which is still moving at a snail's pace. "Come on." he whispers under his breath. Of all the pumps I had to get this one. Suddenly he hears footsteps. "Damn son, you okay?" asks the stranger. Daryl turns his head and looks at the stranger, "Yeah all good, just had a wild night." Fear cuts into his heart like a blade when he sees the stranger. A tall, broad man with a moustache, wearing a button up shirt and boots. "I'd say you did," the stranger replies. Their eyes meet and dread fills them both. Daryl sees a reflection of himself in the man's eyes. "Daryl?" asks the man. "Do you know who I am?" "Yeah I know who you are, Daniel." Daniel looks Daryl up and down and sees the wound on his abdomen, and the bullet holes in the truck. "What the hell did you do this morning Daryl?" he says in a mournful tone. "I didn't mean for things to go this way, I-" "Well what in the hell did you expect to happen?" Daniel asks as his throat tightens, his heartbeat accelerating. "Did you think you were just gonna rob a bank and ride off into the sunset?" "Since when did you give a rat's ass what I do? You got no right to judge me!" Daryl yells with a frail, strained voice. Every breath sends pain through his body, but his anger overrides the sensation. "You killed three people today, you killed a police officer trying to help people." "I didn't want to kill him." "Damn you Daryl, what happened to you son?" Daryl's heart jumps out of his chest, his muscles constrict and his posture stiffens. "YOU left ME, you ran away twenty years ago and left me alone with that devil! And then you want to ask what happened to me!?" Daryl says as he takes a step forward and raises his hands in the air. "Oh so it's my fault you ended up a murderer? When I left home I lived under a bridge for a month, I couldn't even feed myself, let alone you! You were seven years old for God's sake! You wouldn't have made it!" Daryl shakes his head and looks away from Daniel. "All these years and you still can't admit when you're wrong. You know I mourned you. I thought you were dead after you never came back, until I grew up." Daryl says with heavy eyes. Daniel takes a step back and puts his hands on his hips, his heart feeling hollow. "I'm sorry Daryl, I was a stupid kid, I just wanted to get away." Daryl pauses for a moment and catches his breath. He rolls the apology over in his head for a moment. He collects himself and looks Daniel in the eyes. "I don't want your sorry, I'm getting in my truck and leaving, you do what you gotta do Ranger Haze." Daryl takes a step towards the driver's side of the truck. Daniel grits his teeth and shakes his head. "No you're not." Daryl stops and looks at Daniel, his hand resting on his holstered gun. "You gonna shoot your own brother?" Daryl asks. "You killed a good man today. That deputy you killed today was just as much my brother as you are. I'm a man of the law and I got a responsibility to take you in." Daryl snickers and looks at the ground, his mind racing with scenarios of what could happen within the next minute. "You're hurt Daryl, let me take you in, we'll get you in a hospital and get that bullet out of you. I'll make sure you get a fair-" "NO!" Daryl says with a bewildered face, eyes wide, nostrils flared. "I'm not going to prison!" "Please don't be stupid son." Daniel says with sunken eyes and a hesitant voice. "I'm getting in this truck and leaving." Daryl says as he takes another step toward the truck. "Take another step and I'll shoot," Daniel says while gripping his gun tightly, sweat forming on his brow, his hands trying to tremble. Daryl squints his eyes at Daniel and takes two steps away from the truck. "So that's how it's gonna be?"

The two square off under the dim light of the gas station. Lightning still flashes in the distance, hints of moonlight occasionally flicker through the dark clouds, but aside from that, the night is black. Daniel's heart is beating out of his chest as he comes to the realization that he may have to shoot down Daryl. He tries one last time to reason with him. "You're not in your right mind Daryl, you've lost a lot of blood and you're still in shock. Please just come with me," says Daniel. "I'd rather die than get locked up the rest of my life, freedom is the only thing I have left," Daryl says as he rests his hand on his gun. The two stare at each other, hands tightly gripping their weapons. The wind gusts through the night, dark clouds completely cloak the moon from sight now. The lights from the gas station's sign emit a quiet buzzing noise. The wind gusts through again with more ferocity, creating a howling and mourning song. The kind of song that has no definite sound, no real form. A slow winding and changing song that bears no opinion, no judgement. Just indifference. A calm and cold indifference. The wind stops, after what feels like an eternity of waiting, even though it was only a handful of seconds, a miniscule moment, a speck of dust in the spectrum of time, it feels as if decades have passed between seconds.

Daryl's face twitches and his eyes widen, he pulls his gun. POW POW! They fire a single shot on the other almost at the exact same time. Daniel's head whips back and he falls to the ground. Daryl stands in silence for a moment. Click! The pump interrupts the silence as it completes the fueling of Daryl's truck. Daryl then stumbles backwards and doubles over in pain. He takes a deep wheezing breath, and blood spills out of his mouth. Daniel's bullet ripped right through his chest. He drops his gun and falls forward onto his knees and coughs. The front of his white T-shirt is now solid red. He takes a few labored breaths and looks up to the night sky. The colors of the night blur and mix as he begins to fade. He falls onto his face and then rolls onto his back.

Daniel groans and sits up, a small stream of blood trickling down the side of his head. He takes off his cowboy hat which now has a hole in the crown, he feels the wound on the side of his skull where the bullet grazed him. Gun smoke illuminates the night air like dancing spirits. He stands up and stumbles forward, then sways back and finds his balance. His ears ringing and head pounding from the impact, he approaches Daryl who lies motionless, but still breathing. "Hey, Hey, stay with me! Stay with me!" Daryl coughs and spits. Tears spill out of Daniel's eyes as he still tries to make sense of what just happened. Years of pain and trauma stuffed down inside him start to boil out, he can't hold back any longer. His hands are shaking uncontrollably, his heart's ripping apart in his chest. The wind gusts hard across the barren parking lot, blowing right through the broken lawman as he cries for the first time in over a decade. The one light of the station flickers. Daryl's chest is bleeding profusely. Daniel tries to keep pressure on the wound but there's too much blood rushing out. The storm in the distance grows closer, thunder announces its presence in a distant rumble. Daryl grabs Daniel's hands and lift's his head to speak. Daniel leans in to hear him, strong wind tearing through the empty lot. Words escape Daryl's mouth in a whisper, and his head drops back to the ground with his last breath. The light of the gas station flickers, and dies, leaving only the road sign to illuminate the night. Daniel sits back and holds his head in his hands. He never heard Daryl's last words, all he heard was.. Wind.